2023

River,
I hope you
have fun sailing!
through your ABC's.
I love you very much!

Love, ♡

Amber J.

For my husband, Nick-
Let's sail, sail, sail away. - A.J.

N IS FOR NAUTICAL

by Amber Jackson
illustrations Ewa O'Neill

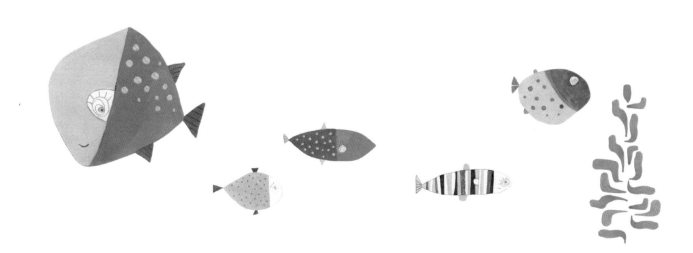

Sail, sail, sail with me
Through your ABC's
Steer the boat left
Then steer it right
We'll sail from A to Z

A is for Anchor

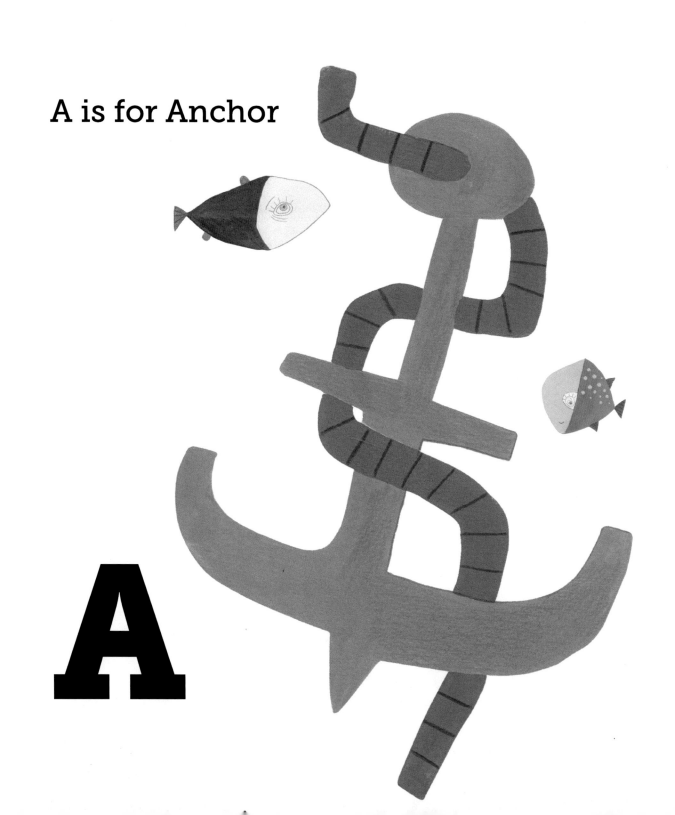

A

B is for Boat

B

C is for Crabs and Clams

D is for Dolphin

D

E is for Ensign

E

F is for Fish

G is for Gusty Winds

G

Sail, sail, sail with me
Through your ABC's
Steer the boat left
Then steer it right
We'll sail from A to Z

H is for Helm

H

And I is for Island

I

J is for Jellyfishes

K is for Kelp

L is for Lighthouse

L

M is for
Mermaid wishes

M

Sail, sail, sail with me
Through your ABC's
Steer the boat left
Then steer it right
We'll sail from A to Z

N is for Net

N

O is for Octopus

P is for Pirates...
Rrrr

P

Q is for Quarterdeck

R is for Ropes

R

S is for Seafarers.

S

Sail, sail, sail with me
Through your ABC's
Steer the boat left
Then steer it right
We'll sail from A to Z

T is for Tugboat

T

U is for Urchin

U

V is for Vessels
Vroom!

V

W for Whale

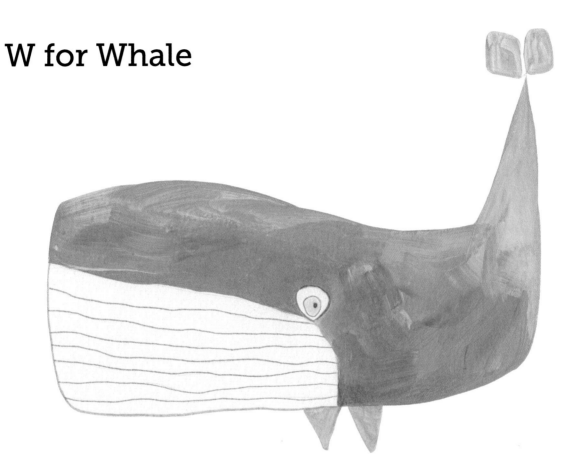

W

X marks the spot

Y is for Yacht

Z is for
Zig
Zag...

Zoom!

Z

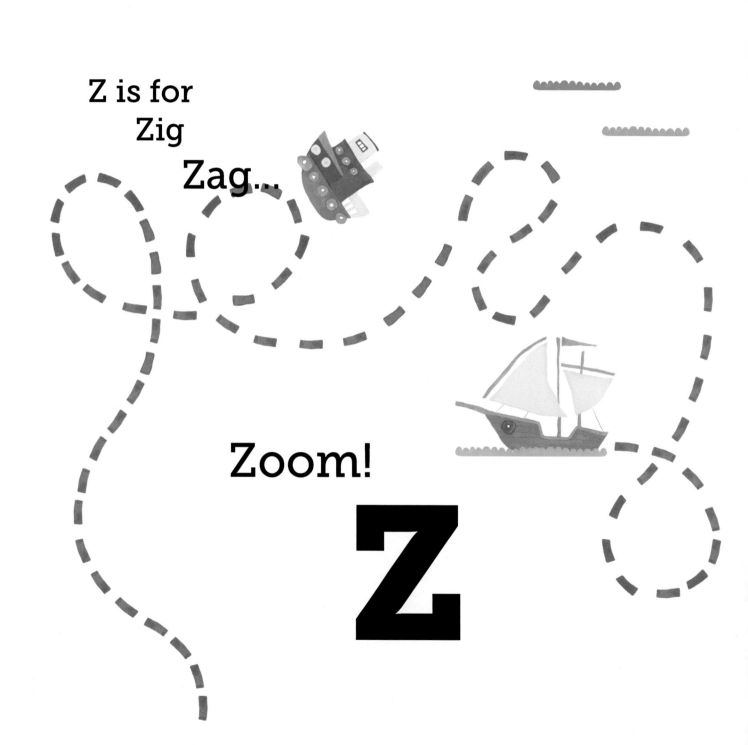

Oh, sail, sail, sail with me
Through your ABC's
Steer the boat left
Then steer it right
We sailed from A to Z

Glossary

Anchor   An anchor helps secure a boat to the bottom of a body of water.

Boat   A boat is a type of watercraft that floats on water.

Clam   A clam is a type of bivalve that typically lives in the shallow areas of seas and oceans.

Crab   A crab is a type of animal that has a hard shell and ten legs. Crabs live in oceans, rivers, lakes, and some even on land.

Dolphin   A dolphin is an aquatic mammal that breathes through a blowhole on top of its head.

Ensign   An ensign is a national flag that is typically flown at the stern of a vessel.

Fish   Fish are cold-blooded animals that use gills to breathe and live entirely in water.

Helm   The helm is the area where the boat is steered.

Island

An island is a body of land completely surrounded by water.

Jellyfish

Jellyfish are marine animals with trailing tentacles and umbrella-shaped bodies. They live in oceans around the world.

Kelp

Kelp are large seaweed that provide food and protection for many fish.

Lighthouse

A lighthouse is a tower that emits light and helps guide people at sea.

Net

A net is used by fishermen to catch fish or other sea animals.

Octopus

An octopus is a type of mollusk with eight arms and a soft body. Octopuses live in all of the world's oceans, but typically enjoy tropical waters.

Quarter Deck

The quarterdeck is located on the upper deck of a vessel. It is set aside by the captain and senior officers for ceremonial and official use.

Seafarer	A seafarer is a person who travels by sea.
Tugboat	A tugboat is a powerful boat that either tugs or pushes larger vessels.
Urchin	A sea urchin is a globular echinoderm covered with sharp, moveable spines.
Vessel	A vessel is any type of ship or boat.
Whale	A whale is a large marine mammal with a blowhole on top of its head for breathing. Whales can be found in all of the world's oceans.
Yacht	A yacht is a type of vessel that is used for recreational purposes.

Made in the USA
Columbia, SC
10 July 2023

20138789R00024